# My Album
## Julia Singing Bear

with Photographs by

Mr. Eldridge McClintock
Mr. Pelham Clarke
and
Julia Singing Bear

Pine Ridge Reservation,
Dakota Territory, 1888

To little Singing Bear who saved my life:

This album is my gift to you for your kindness during my illness, for your grandfather's healing skills, and for your grandmother's beautiful quilled robe that kept me warm this winter.

You have taught me so much about your sacred He Sapa, the mysterious Black Hills. These are the very first photographs ever taken there. Let them speak to you in my white man's way after I have gone. They were created by sunlight. Their captured light will still shine when memory fades.

Eldridge McClintock
Photographer, Black Hills Expedition

April 1875

Pahin

Entering Castle Creek Valley, Black Hills Expedition
with 7th Cavalry under Lt. Colonel Custer, Dakota Territory, 1874

Pte San

Rare White Buffalo in Bison Herd

*Red Willow, Montana Territory, Yellowstone River, 1872*

My English name is Julia but I am called Singing Bear. I am Oglala of the Lakota Sioux. My father was Tall Bear and my mother was Butterfly Woman, daughter of Red Feather, holy man of our people. I was born in the Year of the Hundred Slain.

In the fall when I was two winters, some of our people went to hunt buffalo along the Arikaree River with the Cheyenne of Chief Roman Nose. My mother and father were among them. The herds were hungry for the blue stem grass and were running fast to the plains. I was too little to make such a journey horseback. I stayed in the green quiet world surrounding the He Sapa with my grandmother and grandfather.

Each day I looked for my parents to appear with buffalo meat and stories of their hunt. After the Moon of the Bitter Cold, we learned that they would not return. They and the others had been killed by soldiers. Grandmother cut my hair and we cried together during the winter snows remembering my mother and father.

Wanbli

*Golden Eagle Flying over Black Hills, 1874*

When I was old enough, Grandmother took me with her to find porcupines for her quill work. Grandmother was a master worker. She found her designs in dreams that Double Faced Woman sent to her. She showed me the difficult stitches she made on our robes and moccasins, and she taught me the meaning of her designs.

One day, following signs of a porcupine near our camp, we found a young bear cub with quills in his snout. The cub rolled and yelped in pain. Grandmother pulled out the

quills and brought the little cub back home to be my brother. I called him Matocinca, which means the bear child in my language. We played together in the summers in the forests, by the hot springs and on the rocks. He showed me how to dig for roots. We picked berries and ate until our stomachs were round. He climbed up into the bee trees and brought me sticky honey. We roamed the hills side by side. Grandmother knew I was safe with Matocinca.

On summer mornings Matocinca scratched at our tipi with his sharp curved claws. Then I would creep out with Grandfather to sing the morning song to the Great Spirit. Sometimes Matocinca sang with us in his deep growl.

Lakota Girl in Ceremonial Dress, Black Hills, 1874

My friend Singing Bear

When I was four winters, I was honored to become hunka, a child beloved. There was a sacred hunka ceremony, and Grandmother painted my face with many tiny red lines. Bear Shield was my hunka ate, my adopting father, and I became a part of his family. For the honoring ceremony, Grandmother made me a dress with two hundred elk teeth sewn on it. That dress was worth many horses.

Whenever we killed the elk for their meat, horns and hides, we also took their teeth. The teeth last forever. We used the two milk teeth to decorate our clothes. We offered tobacco to thank the elk for their gifts. The piles of elk horns we made showed our respect for these shadow friends who hide in the woods.

The wasicun, the white men, loved to kill four-leggeds—deer, antelope, beaver, bear and elk. They did not know that all animals could talk with us and give us their powers. I was afraid that a wasicun might kill my brother Matocinca.

He Haka

*Elk Horn Pile near Bear Butte, Dakota Territory, 1874*

One summer a long line of white men on tall horses rode into the He Sapa. Matocinca and I hid behind the pines and rocks and watched the wagons roll through the valley. There were hundreds of soldiers with many mules, dogs and small spotted buffalo. Their shouts and songs frightened all the animals in the hills. I saw the headman with the long yellow hair and his scouts. These men had not come to the He Sapa to find tipi poles, herbs or porcupines. Grandfather said these men had come to steal from our hills.

In the mornings two of the white men took the tallest wagon and rode off alone. I named the driver Black Boots and the other man Hat. I followed them. Every day they went to a different place in the hills and stopped. From the wagon they took a big black Box and stood it on three short tipi poles. Then Hat would cover his head and the back of the Box with a dark blanket and hide there. After a few minutes he would throw off the blanket and pull a clear flat square from the Box. He would run back to the wagon holding the square and disappear inside.

His hands turned black. At first I thought Hat was doing a secret ceremony under the blanket. Now I know he was pulling the sunlight into his Box to make pictures for the army expedition.

Custer Long Hair

Setting out from Fort Lincoln for Black Hills Expedition,
Dakota Territory, July 1874

After a time all the loud men moved off, led by Long Hair. I believed we were safe when our hills were silent once more. Grandfather prayed to protect us from the soldiers. He knew they would come again.

It was the season to gather plants for paints and medicine herbs. We left our camp circle to look for yellow pine and larkspur. Soon after we saw the tall wagon return alone, carrying Hat, Black Boots and a Crow scout. The first night they camped by the creek in the valley. The next day they drove the wagon to the base of the highest rocky peak overlooking the valley. Matocinca and I tracked each move they made, stopping when they stopped. Their scout had lazy eyes. He did not see us.

Tunkasila

Sioux Medicine Man, Black Hills Expedition,
Dakota Territory, 1874

Wapostan

Hat climbed up with his Box to the tallest rock. He placed the Box on the little tipi poles at the very edge and looked down into the valley. A great thundercloud moved swiftly over us and I felt the rushing wind. Hat was under the black blanket and he did not notice the storm coming behind him. In one angry breath the winds blew Hat over the cliff and down into the bushes near where we were standing. Then the clouds burst. Lightning flashed and rains fell. I thought the Great Powers were punishing Hat for entering our sacred hills. I ran out from behind the trees and called to Scout. I signed to him that my grandfather was a holy man and a healer. Scout signed back and asked for help. I ran for Grandfather.

When we returned Hat was as silent as death. His leg was broken. Grandfather quickly set the bones and wrapped Hat's leg in a green deer hide with wooden splints. Then Grandfather sang his healing song. We placed Hat in his wagon and moved it next to our tipi.

This was the way I met Hat, the man I now know as Eldridge McClintock, the photographer of the 1874 Black Hills Army Expedition, who became my friend.

*Travelling Dark Room with Cicero Bland and Jeb Tackett,*
*Box Elder Creek, Black Hills, Dakota Territory, August 1874*

Each summer lightning fires raged through the He Sapa, frightening all the animals and leaving dark scars on the green woodland. We called these fires red buffalo. The thunderwind that blew Hat down to us started such a blaze. It travelled in a fury, roaring through the hills and out onto the prairie, cutting us off from our people. Hat could not be moved. We told Scout and Black Boots to return in a few moons when Hat's leg had healed. We would care for him.

Hat slept for many days. I knew he would live, for Grandfather had great powers. The green hide hardened stiff and strong. The Great Spirit must have been pleased with Hat to save his precious Box and glass plates and to put me, Matocinca and my grandparents right where he fell.

When Hat awoke, he found me studying his magic Box and the grey pictures he kept in his tall wagon. They were strange pictures—exactly what my eyes saw when I looked at the He Sapa, but small and without color. It looked as if everything in them had been dusted with ash from the great fire.

Tatokala

*Pronghorn Antelope in Black Hills, 1874*

*Forest Fire at Camp*

*Montana Territory, 1867*

Hat was frightened to see a bear standing at the entrance to his wagon. He did not yet know the power bears have to heal. While Hat was with us, I taught him much about our life in the He Sapa. Hat taught me much too. As time passed he taught me white man's words, and I spoke to him in Lakota. He grew used to my bear brother.

Hat stayed in his wagon next to our tipi until he could hobble about. By this time winter had come. Hat could not make photographs. No one could move the studio wagon in the deep snow. No one could run from the Box with the wet plate fast enough. But it was a good time for me to learn how to make a photograph. Hat let me go under the black cloth and look through the eyes of the large heavy Box he called Camera. Camera's eyes saw every thing upside down. Hat also had a small one-eyed Camera for people pictures. He had used that one to photograph Long Hair with his scout and a grizzly bear they had shot.

I told Hat I liked pictures with live animals better than pictures with dead animals. He laughed and said that he would take a picture of me with Matocinca, a live girl and a live bear. When Matocinca came back from his winter sleep, Hat took a picture of me with my brother. I liked that picture best of all.

Long Hair

Scout

Matohota

Grizzly Bear Hunt near Bear Butte, 1874

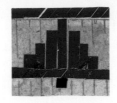

Hat showed me a picture he had made of the Cheyenne captives taken at the
Washita River. They were women and little children. He told me he had been with
Long Hair when he attacked a Cheyenne camp six winters before he came to the
Black Hills. He told me the headman, Black Kettle, had been promised safety as
long as the starred spangle banner flew over his village. Long Hair and his soldiers
did not respect this promise. Black Kettle and his wife, Medicine Woman, were shot
by wasicun crossing the Washita. More than a hundred Cheyenne were killed,
and all of the horses, mules and dogs. The village was burned to the ground.
This was the same winter my parents were killed by soldiers.

I think Hat was ashamed of what happened to the Cheyenne. All of their families
were broken. The little children were taken far away and put in prison.
They had nothing to wear but blankets. Hat's picture showed their sorrow.

*Prisoners from Battle of the Washita, Fort Hayes, Kansas, 1868*

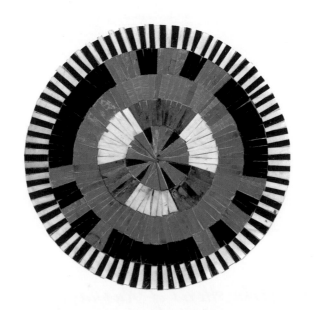

Hat told me that Duke and the white men danced with our people before the buffalo hunt. In this dance picture I saw Bear Shield, White Bull and Iron Arm, the headman of our people.

After the hunt, Duke sat at a wooden table he had brought with him and ate quail eggs. He drank minipiga, a pale gold drink with bubbles. He drank from a tall thin cup made of glass, like the glass plates Hat used for making photographs. Hat told me Duke did not eat the meat of the buffalo he killed, only the tongue.

I had been on many buffalo hunts myself. The women were always nearby as the men chased the herds. We were all of us there to work, not to play. The more buffalo killed, the harder we worked, cutting, stripping, and drying meat.

White Bull

Bear Shield

Iron Arm

Buffalo Dance of the Sioux Warriors, North Platte, January 1872

Hat showed me many photographs of buffalo herds. In one picture I saw he had photographed a white buffalo. I have never seen a real white buffalo, only the wooly animals covered with snow in the winter. I told Hat the story of White Buffalo Calf Woman who brought us the pipe and the seven ceremonies that taught us how to live. White Buffalo Calf Woman was the messenger from the spirits to the Lakota people.

Hat learned great respect for the buffalo, wrapped as he was during that cold in warm, furry hides with Grandmother's finest quilled robe on top. He saw that we were part of the family of creatures that came from the earth. The twin eyes in Hat's Box took in the bigness and the wholeness of our world. This was a new way of seeing for a white army photographer, used to living in cramped, square towns with no space, no sky, and no four-leggeds for relatives.

By the time the snows had melted, Hat was well again. In the Moon of Thunderstorms, Black Boots and Scout came back for him, bringing spare horses. We gave Hat gifts. In return, he gave us four of the big white man horses, coffee, sugar, and shiny tin pots for cooking. For me he had a special gift—this album and some of the photographs I liked best.

Tatanka

*Sparring Bison, Wyoming Territory, 1872*

*Headquarters of the Black Hills Expedition below Harney Peak*

*Hidden Wood Creek, Dakota Territory, July 8, 1874*

Two winters after Hat left, in the Moon of Making Fat, Sitting Bull, a Hunkpapa, called all the Lakota peoples and the Cheyenne and the Arapahoe to come to a ceremony at Deer Medicine Rocks. Grandfather was to help in the preparation for the Sun Dance. We travelled west many days, passing the sacred place where the tree stump rose up to the heavens to protect Lakota children from an angry bear. His claw marks scarred the giant stump and it turned to stone. The children became stars.

The purpose of the Sun Dance was to sacrifice before the holy tree in thanksgiving, and to ask the Great Powers to look upon the dancers with favor in the coming year. Thousands joined us for this ceremony. Sitting Bull loosened his hair and made many wounds on his body. He danced all day and all night and the next day. Before he fainted, he whispered his vision to Black Moon. Sitting Bull said that he had seen soldiers falling with their heads down right into our camp. The vision told that the soldiers who wanted war were coming straight to the river called the Greasy Grass and would be killed there.

Mato Tipi

The Devil's Tower, Montana Territory, 1874

Grandfather said more white soldiers would come to kill us. So our people rode back to the east, leaving the dead lying in the fields above the Greasy Grass. Grandfather said this battle was not what it seemed. It was not a good beginning. It would have a bad end.

On the way back, near the He Sapa, we were attacked by Crow warriors. Our men were out searching for buffalo, yet we held the Crow off until Iron Arm and our hunters returned. Grandfather rushed out to protect us. The leader of the Crow war party rode up behind Grandfather and snatched away his sacred medicine pouch. Grandfather ran after him, but the Crow turned and fired his long gun. Grandfather staggered and fell. Then he lay still. The enemies rode away.

I could not stay silent. I wailed with the pain of my sorrow. Grandmother too was stricken with grief. We cut off our hair and slashed our arms. Then I sang a song of Red Feather, my grandfather. I imagined how his spirit would fly away like the geese and the trumpeting swans, the blue swallows and the eagles. The red hawk feathers he wore showed he was one with the wingeds. I prayed that his wise spirit would always remember me.

Unci

Sioux Woman, Black Hills Expedition, Dakota Territory, 1874

We gave away all of our household items, including Hat's tin pots and even our tipi that Grandfather had painted. We were in mourning. This is the way of my people. In four days our people provided us with new possessions to start our new lives.

At Gathering Mountain, we placed Grandfather on a scaffold so he could go to the spirit world. We wrapped him in his most beautiful robe, decorated with a spiderweb design. The web stood for the heavens, the four directions, the winds, and the thunders. Thunder is spider's friend. We placed the white man's looking glass beside Grandfather to flash power at anyone who came to disturb him. I sang my Bear song and asked Matocinca to guard Grandfather.

I knew I could live with Bear Shield, my hunka-ate, and his family, and that he would provide for Grandmother and me. He had sworn to give his life for me. I was his relative and he mine. Grandmother and I went into the hills to find porcupines for quilling. We wanted to make moccasins and clothes with beautiful stories on them for our new family. We went to live with Bear Shield at Pine Ridge Reservation.

Sioux Burial Scaffold, Montana Territory, 1872

That winter was very cruel. The wasicun promised us food and blankets. They did not bring the food, and their blankets gave no warmth. There were no buffalo to hunt. At the Agency store, Grandmother traded her quill and bead work for the food we needed. Her designs were greatly valued. She helped feed all of Bear Shield's children.

Grandmother became the head of the quilling society at the Reservation. It was an honor to belong. Often the quill workers came to our tipi. I watched them work and helped Grandmother cook food for them. The women spoke of fighting, of Crazy Horse and Sitting Bull, and of the white man town called Custer, named for the dead Long Hair. It was located in the middle of our hills, near the place where Hat fell down to me.

When summer came, we went with some of our people to the edge of the He Sapa to find prairie turnips. We dug them out of the earth with sharp sticks and braided them into strings. In the winter we would use them for soups and stews. We passed by Grandfather's burial place and gathered his bones and set stones on top. Matocinca had been faithful. No one had disturbed Grandfather.

One morning when Grandmother and I were digging far from the
others, three wasicun rode up on horseback. They laughed at
Grandmother and called her a bear woman, a digger of roots. They
threw a rope around her and dragged her over the rocky ground.
I rushed at the men with my digging stick. I knocked the rope man from
his horse and freed Grandmother. The men chased me so I struck their horses with my
sharp stick. Then Iron Arm rode up, and the white men galloped away. Grandmother said
she feared for me. I had been honored to become hunka. In exchange, I had taken special
vows of purity and generosity. She did not think I would be safe any longer in the hills with
wild wasicun looking for Indians to hunt and kill.

Not long after, when I was thirteen winters, a soldier called Lieutenant Bruce came to the
Reservation. With him was a pretty white lady, Miss Marcy, who spoke Lakota. I used white
man words to tell them about the men who tried to hurt Grandmother. Miss Marcy said
she wanted to take me with Bear Shield's children to a school in the East to
learn about civilization and education. Grandmother liked education
and Lieutenant Bruce's words about how safe I would be at the school
in Pennsylvania. She was not sure about civilization.

Suzanne Medicine Water

Alice Eliza Silver Heels

Leslie Two Goats

Malova Good Woman

First Class at Carlisle Indian School

Konrad Blue Sky

Thomas Blue Eagle

Yellow Bird

Henry Tall Tree

Carlisle, Pennsylvania, 1879

We arrived at Carlisle town on a cold, grey day. The school had been an army camp for over one hundred winters. There was no place in the buildings for fires, and there was very little to eat. We spoke with the children from other tribes in sign.

Carl Loloma

By day we were brave. At night we cried to ourselves. We were afraid. We did not know what was right or wrong. When we disobeyed orders, we were shut up in the stone guardhouse. We had become like the prisoners of the Washita, without fathers or headmen to lead us.

We had come to be with the white people and to learn how they lived. I hoped we would find teachers like Hat and Miss Marcy who would be kind to us.

I was fortunate Hat had given me English. I helped teach the children white man's words, and they respected me for my good speaking. I learned writing. After a time we received things from the Great White Father—clothes, shoes, beds, and stoves. We played ball on the parade ground and were allowed to slide on the icy river. I began to make friends. There was Blue Eagle, who had travelled with me from Pine Ridge. At Carlisle I picked the English name Thomas for him, and I chose the name Julia for myself.

And there was Yellow Bird, who also knew English words and how to write them. He was Cheyenne, but not full blood. He told me that his mother had been taken prisoner at the Washita.

The headman, Captain Pratt, was proud of his Indian school. He hired a photographer, Mr. Pelham Clarke. Later Miss Marcy arranged for me to help him for 50¢ each week. Like Hat, he had a studio wagon where he made his pictures. He used dry plates, not wet ones, so my hands did not turn black. His Camera was different and his pictures looked different too. They were very solemn.

One picture showed all of the school staff. Some of them had mean faces. Dr. Sterrett, who had bushy black whiskers, called us savage and stupid. It was he who ordered our hair cut and had us scrubbed with soap. He threw away our Indian clothes. The only Lakota thing I could keep was the sewing bag that held my quills.

Lt. Bruce
Mr. Shoemaker
Miss Evans
Dr. Sterrett
Miss Marcy
Miss Nila

Each school day we marched through the iron gate out on to the parade grounds. We wore uniforms and sang a spangle banner song. Then we went to class to learn education. In the afternoon we worked to learn trades—cooking, washing, cleaning, sewing. The boys learned horsecare, shoemaking, carpentry, tinsmithing, printing. We had little time to think about our families far away.

I was beginning to feel pulled in two different directions like Double Faced Woman.

  I had quilled in the Indian way. Now I was embroidering in the white way. Mrs. Pratt liked my designs. I am sure Double Faced Woman came to Mrs. Pratt in dreams too, but she did not understand Lakota and could not translate her dreams into designs. Mrs. Pratt's embroidery was just tangled flowers.

Anog Ite

The sewing class was like our quilling and beading society meetings, but without food. We told stories as we worked and followed white women's patterns from magazines. These patterns were named fashions, meaning something to make. And we did make and make and make. We made clothes for all the hundreds of children at the school. We made other things too— knickers for girls and shirts Captain Pratt sold to the army. I made a warm coat for the youngest child, Sampson Fire, a little Apache boy of four winters. It looked just like the great coat Captain Pratt wore with soldier buttons and epaulettes.

  I was proud of my white man's clothing.

*Sewing Class, 1880   Alice Eliza Silver Heels, Leslie Two Goats*

We also learned graciousness and culture. These were important for civilization. That meant art and music. Captain Pratt wanted us to make art with charcoal. We were told to copy dishes, flowers, bowls. We stood up as we drew and tried to put down just what we saw. It was like bad photographs without Camera. Mr. Clarke could do it just as well for 25¢. One boy made fine wasicun pictures and painted them with beautiful colors. Some were pale like rainbow colors, made with water. Others were bright like dream colors, made with oily paint. The boy was a Crow named Henry Tall Tree and he was very unfriendly. Thomas Blue Eagle made pictures in the Lakota way when Captain Pratt was not looking.

Madge Little Plume

I showed my photograph album to Captain Pratt and Mr. Clarke. Mr. Clarke liked Hat's pictures very much. He gave me photographs to add to my collection. He even let me take some photographs myself because he was very busy shooting all the Indian befores and afters when new children arrived. First they were shot in their Indian clothes. Then they were shot in the woolen white man clothes we made at the school.

Our music teacher, Miss Perry, explained how to write down the music sounds to make a song. The marks were little circles with tails and they made tracks on the lined paths that travelled across the pages. She showed us how to follow these paths on the piano, a kind of wooden table with little black and white boards called keys. The boards made sounds like voices singing when you pressed them with your fingers. You could also follow the path with your own voice and sing the notes. Miss Perry said I sang like a bird. She taught us a song about a mockingbird and a French song about a bird called "Alouette." She taught us another French song called "Frère Jacques."

Miss Perry and Rosa Looks Back

Miss Marcy asked me to help Henry Tall Tree with English. I did not want to teach him anything. He was always making trouble and being punished. He worked with the horses because he could talk to them. They were his only friends. Sometimes Mr. Clarke let Tall Tree drive the photography wagon.

One day all the boys went camping with Lieutenant Bruce. That night Blue Eagle returned to the school alone. He was bleeding. He told me that he and Tall Tree had fought over a medicine pouch and Tall Tree had stabbed him with something sharp. Blue Eagle handed the pouch to me. It was my grandfather's medicine pouch.

I took the sacred things from the pouch and touched them to Blue Eagle. I prayed to the Great Powers to heal him. Soon the bleeding stopped and the wound closed. I thanked the Great Powers for bringing the pouch and its healing ways to me. I told Blue Eagle that we must perform a peace ceremony with Tall Tree. I saw now that it was a new time for all of us. Together the three of us smoked the pipe. I started in earnest to help Tall Tree with English words. We worked well together. I told him about Grandmother's blanket. I asked him to make a color map of the pictures I wanted to embroider on it showing my life at Carlisle School. He was happy to help me.

Henry Tall Tree

In my second autumn at school, Captain Pratt had a special dinner. It was a celebration the white people held each year to give thanks. We ate roasted turkey, redberry sauce, and a dark sweet called chocolate on frozen cream. We wore our prettiest clothes. I made a dress from silk cloth I had purchased with my photography money. When I touched it, the silk made a noise like leaves rustling in the wind. It looked wet and shiny like a river.

My Silk Dress

The dress was fashioned from a pattern I found in Harper's magazine. I embroidered the sleeves and used pearl buttons. They cost me three dollars. When I looked at my reflection in the mirror, I was just like the fine white ladies in the magazine. I felt pretty. After the dinner I danced with Tall Tree and Blue Eagle in the white man's way. We did Polka and Waltz. I liked this different way of dancing.

Sometimes we went on outings, and we lived in the homes of white people. We learned English faster that way. We also learned manners and how to take tea. I wore my pretty dress for tea parties too.

Minda Long Feather and Fred Redwater, Cornelius Night Pipe and Josie Raven,
Richard Spotted Horse, Eric Whistler, Bridget Little Star and Abe Lincoln

One day Captain Pratt took us to a circus. This was a special day because we did not have school or work. Lieutenant Bruce marched us into town and into a great tipi with stripes. We sat on wooden benches in a circle. We ate sweet candy and peanuts. We heard the drums. Then the torches were lit. Pretty ladies in short sparkle dresses rode out on dancing horses. Then acrobats climbed on each others' shoulders and jumped about like the flying squirrels in the He Sapa. A girl hung by her knees from a swing at the top of the tipi and then swooped like a hawk into the arms of a man below. A boy holding a parasol walked on a rope like a mountain goat. It was wonderful! There were tumbling clowns, and at the end, a bear. He had on a collar of stars, and he danced around in a circle when his keeper played the hand piano.

The bear reminded me of Matocinca and of the star children above Mato Tipi. Suddenly, Matocinca appeared to me in a dream vision. His face came up from a pool of hot bubbles. He wore a wreath of blackberries. I climbed on his back and he jumped over a rocky ridge. Then he disappeared. I did not understand this vision, but I knew it was a message for me. I missed Matocinca and my Grandmother.

Peabody Brothers Circus, March 13, 1883

Often when I worked for Mr. Clarke I would play with Rufus, his little son. He had a toy that was called Kaleidoscope. It was a long tube with pieces of colored looking glass in it. It had a Camera eye, only inside it saw colors and patterns and they moved. In the dreams Double Faced Woman sent me there were different colors and patterns that moved about just like that toy. I saw symbols from the quill designs on robes and moccasins and pictures the men painted of horses and buffalo. They swirled about and gave me messages. I embroidered these dream patterns on Grandmother's blanket.

One day Bear Shield visited the school again and told Captain Pratt he was taking his children home. Captain Pratt agreed to let them go if I stayed on to help with the English teaching. I told Bear Shield that I would stay at Carlisle for two more winters. I had two new brothers, Tall Tree and Blue Eagle, and I did not want to leave them.

Bear Shield

Tall Tree, Blue Eagle and I could not forget our lives on the Plains. Together we had little ceremonies and said prayers in secret, away from Captain Pratt and Dr. Sterrett. We were white in the light and Indian in the dark.

Captain Pratt and Dr. Sterrett believed our customs were
 wrong, our clothes were wrong, our gods were wrong, and our
medicines were wrong. Being right meant being just like
 them. But I was not like them. I was an Oglala and a
relative of White Buffalo Calf Woman. I had tried to follow
 their white ways. I even liked some of these ways. Still
I could not change all my Indian ways, even if it meant
 I would never be civilized.

Jesse Frog

Dr. Sterrett ordered me to help in the infirmary where sick children went. He needed
 someone who could comfort the little ones. It was the only time I was allowed to speak
Lakota. Dr. Sterrett watched me closely. His black whiskers followed me about.

In the pharmacy there were rows of glass bottles with medicines in them like the ones in
 the surgeon's case I had found at the Greasy Grass. Many times I had to plead with sick
children to take these white man medicines. They feared the strange liquids. When
 Dr. Sterrett was not in the room, I would say Indian prayers with the children.

Nurses at the Hospital, Carlisle Indian School

Soon after I began helping in the infirmary, several children at the school fell ill with a bad stomach disease. Dr. Sterrett thought that they were eating tobacco or practicing savage ceremonies. He got this foolish idea from inspecting my grandfather's medicine pouch. Miss Marcy told me he had come to our rooms and looked at all the Indian keepsakes. In my pouch were Grandfather's little pipe, tobacco leaves, powdered herbs, roots and feathers. It was a sacred bundle. I told Lieutenant Bruce, who understood Indian ways. He had angry words with Dr. Sterrett. Lieutenant Bruce demanded that he leave my pouch alone. He said, "We have taken enough away from our Indian children."

More and more children fell ill, and adults too. There was no room left in the infirmary. Some of my friends died and were buried in the ground in a little cemetery there at Carlisle. At night I went with Blue Eagle and Tall Tree and placed tobacco bundles in the trees next to their gravestones. Mr. Clarke's son Rufus became sick too. Mr. and Mrs. Clarke were very frightened. None of the children got better. My Cheyenne friend Yellow Bird was so weak he could barely talk to me. He begged me to use Lakota medicine to help him. I made a prayer for his recovery.

The Hospital, Carlisle Indian School

Finally I knew what my bear vision meant. I remembered that once, when I was small, I became very sick from drinking standing water. Grandfather boiled the roots of the blackberry bush and told me to drink the root water. It made me well.

The cure for the sickness at Carlisle was to stop drinking from the wells and to get fresh water. Blackberry root tea would help settle the sick children's stomachs. This was the message Matocinca sent by the dancing bear to help Yellow Bird and Rufus Clarke.

I called to Tall Tree and Blue Eagle and told them about my vision. I knew where to find some blackberries. We could go to Boiling Springs, a town not far from school.

During my first summer at Carlisle I had stayed in Boiling Springs with Mr. and Mrs. Carl Frederick. The Fredericks were friends of Mr. Clarke. They were preparing to move to Custer, the new white man's mining town in the Black Hills. I liked telling them about the He Sapa, the pines and the animals. They were very kind to me.

They taught me to bake bread and make blackberry jam and pies. We had picnics near Boiling Springs and filled our baskets with blackberries. I remembered the place well.

Mrs. Clarke with Rufus James and Mr. Pelham Clarke at a Picnic
at Boiling Springs with Mr. and Mrs. Carl Frederick

Tall Tree, Blue Eagle and I made a plan. Tall Tree would get Whirlwind, the horse he used to drive the photography wagon. Blue Eagle would get a kettle and some tin containers with lids. I would get Mr. Clarke's tripod. At midnight, Tall Tree would make bird calls outside my window and together we would ride to Boiling Springs where the blackberries grew. Blue Eagle would be the scout hiding in the cemetery next to the stables, ready to warn us when we returned if there was trouble.

Mr. Clarke did not notice that I had not put the tripod back in the wagon that evening. When it grew dark I waited by the window. Finally, I heard Tall Tree's calls. I climbed out onto the balcony and slid down the pillar. Tall Tree had painted Whirlwind in a sacred way, like a warrior preparing for battle. He used the dragonfly design to make us invisible. We both climbed on Whirlwind and I held on tight to Tall Tree. We jumped over the low stone fence and galloped to Boiling Springs.

We reached the springs and gathered blackberries and the stem roots in the moonlight. I set up the tripod and hung the kettle from it. Tall Tree made a fire. The water cooked the roots and berries. We quickly filled the tins and put the lids on tight. We wrapped the tins in a blanket so they would not clank. Then we raced back to the cemetery.

No one had missed us. As soon as it was light, I tucked a tin under my apron. I hid another tin in my knickers. I walked over to the infirmary to see Yellow Bird. I gave him a container of the root drink and left the other tin under his bed. I told him to drink it all as soon as he could, before Dr. Black Whiskers found it. I gave the same blackberry tea to Mrs. Clarke. I explained that this medicine had healed me when I had stomach sickness in the Black Hills. She trusted me and our Indian medicine. She was willing to try anything to help her son Rufus.

Henry Tall Tree

Soon both Yellow Bird and Rufus were better. Mrs. Clarke demanded that Captain Pratt change the water supply. He sent army wagons over to Boiling Springs for fresh water for all the children. The sickness passed. Mr. and Mrs. Clarke were so grateful to me for healing Rufus. They said I would receive a very special graduation present after I had returned to the Reservation. They gave me a letter to the Fredericks, who were now in Custer town, asking them to give me employment when I returned to the Dakota Territory.

My six years at Carlisle had passed quickly. I was excited to be going home to Pine Ridge with Thomas Blue Eagle. Still I was pulled in two directions. I looked forward to seeing Grandmother and my brother Matocinca. But I was sad to leave my school friends and teachers, and I knew that I would miss helping Mr. Clarke in his studio.

Thomas Blue Eagle

Mr. Clarke's photograph of me at work in his studio, Carlisle, Pennsylvania

When I returned home to Pine Ridge I gave Grandmother the blanket that told my story. I showed her my album with the Carlisle pictures added to it. She said she had been with me all the time and had seen these pictures in her dreams.

I was happy to work for Mr. and Mrs. Frederick in their store. I used the skills I had learned with Mrs. Pratt to make clothes for the white people in Custer town. The townspeople liked my fashionable dresses and coats. I was able to take good care of Grandmother and all of Bear Shield's family with the money I earned. I visited them every month at Pine Ridge, since they could not leave the Reservation without a permit.

During one visit Thomas Blue Eagle brought me a box wrapped in brown paper that had been sent to the Pine Ridge Agent. Inside the box was a note from Mrs. Clarke and another box that said Julia. This one was tied with a pink silk ribbon. I could not wait to open it.

My surprise was a new type of Camera. It was named Kodak. This camera used film to catch the sun. It did not need a wet plate or a wagon. You could take many pictures one after another and then send the film away to get the photographs. The Clarkes asked me to send them pictures from the Black Hills.

Custertown 1888

I was the only Indian in the Black Hills who had a Kodak. Everyone who visited Custer town wanted pictures of Indians. It made me proud to pose my people in their beautiful quilled and beaded clothes for my photographs. I saw how wonderful their robes were, finer by far than the dresses and plain woolen coats I made for the white people to wear. These robes spoke for themselves.

I took many pictures of Grandmother wrapped in the embroidered story blanket I had made for her. When the film came back, Kodak had made her face look wrinkled and ridged like the rocky hills in the He Sapa. She did not look that way in real life to me.

The next summer we went to Grandfather's burial place and returned his medicine pouch. I put it next to his bones. When I sang a song to Grandfather, Matocinca appeared and I greeted him. He was my healing bear who had saved my friends.

# About the Art of Quilling

When visitors from Europe first arrived in the New World in the seventeenth century, they were prepared for wild and rugged country. They were not prepared for the magnificently decorated clothing worn by the native people. The use of the porcupine quill to beautify tanned hides was a unique North American art form practiced only by women. It was difficult work, requiring great dexterity, patience in preparation, and artistic vision. To the Lakota, quilling was a sacred gift from the Double Faced Woman, Anog Ite, a legendary dream figure. The designs she inspired were symbolic and served as messengers between the natural and spirit worlds.

Before use, quills were colored with vegetable dyes. Then they were sorted. The coarsest came from the tail of the porcupine and the finest from the belly.

Variations in the size of the quill enhanced the design. The quillworker held several quills in her mouth when embroidering, softening them with saliva to make them pliable. The quills were folded over sinew to form patterns and held in place with a stitch. The arrangement of color and size made for bold or delicate designs.

Some would say the buffalo hunters and warriors of the Plains are legends of the American West, overshadowing their women. But this sisterhood left a vibrant and indelible record of their lives. Their stories were transmitted by their fingers into quill designs of great artistry, which are highly valued by collectors, galleries, and museums all over the world. Lakota women of today continue this great tradition.

# About the Early Days of Photography

Photography literally means writing with light. It was discovered in the early nineteenth century as the result of a combination of three principles—linear perspective, projection by means of the camera obscura, and certain chemicals that turned dark when exposed to light.

In the early days of photography, all of the many operations, from composing the picture to developing it, were carried out by the photographers themselves in their own darkrooms. During the 1870s, adventurous and talented photographers roamed the "uninhabited" territories of the West. They worked under arduous conditions, travelling with cumbersome materials. It was a craft for skilled technicians with strong constitutions. In this same period, George Eastman recognized the opportunity to make photography available to the amateur and developed the Kodak box camera, which used film instead of dry plates. He finally registered the word "Kodak" in 1888 and mass marketed his new camera. It became an instant success.

The paintings in this book are based in part on photographs taken in the 1870s and 1880s by William F. Illingworth and John N. Choate. Illingworth accompanied Custer on the Black Hills Geological Expedition of 1874 and took many photographs there. Copies of his original photographs still exist in the United States Army archives and at the South Dakota Historical Society. Choate was the first of several photographers at the Carlisle Indian Industrial School, and many of his original glass plates are at the Cumberland County Historical Society in Carlisle, Pennsylvania.

# Glossary

| Lakota Word | Pronunciation | English Meaning |
|---|---|---|
| Anog Ite | ah-NO-gee-day (g as in "dog") | Double Faced Woman |
| Hehaka | hay-CHAH-KAH (ch is in the throat, as in the German word "achtung") | Male elk |
| He Sapa | CHAY-sah-pah (ch as in "achtung") | Black Hills |
| Hunkpapa | HOONK-pah-pah | A tribe of the Lakota |
| Hunka | hoonk-GAH | Child Beloved |
| Hunka Ate | hoonk-GAH-ah-DAY | Adopting father |
| Matocinca | MAH-toe-cheen-cha (ch as in "cherry") | Bear Child |
| Mato Hota | MAH-TOE-choh-dah (ch as in "achtung") | Grizzly bear |
| Mato Tipi | MAH-TOE-tee-pee | Bear's Lodge |
| Minipiga | min-nee-BEE-GAH | Beer |
| Pahin | pah-HEE | Porcupine |
| Pte San | ptay-SAH | White female buffalo |
| Tatanka | TAW-tunk-ah (taw sounds like "saw") | Male buffalo |
| Tatokala | tah-TOE-kah-la | Pronghorn antelope |
| Tunkasila | toong-KAH-shee-la | Grandfather |
| Unci | oon-chee (ch as in "cherry") | Grandmother |
| Wakanyeja | wah-KAHN-yah-ja (the j sounds like the soft s in "fusion") | Children |
| Wanbli | wahn-BLEE | Eagle |
| Wapostan | waw-POE-shduh (waw sounds like "saw") | Hat |
| Wasicun | waw-SHEE-choo (waw sounds like "saw") | White man |

NOTE: Capitalized syllables should be emphasized. Because there are some sounds in Lakota that cannot be duplicated in English, these pronunciations are approximate.

# The Journal of Julia Singing Bear

Jewel Grutman and Gay Matthaei, authors
Adam Cvijanovic, artist

created in consultation with
Arthur Amiotte, a Lakota Studies professor
and Oglala Lakota tribal member

This book is a companion to THE LEDGERBOOK OF THOMAS BLUE EAGLE.
The story is a work of fiction based on historical fact.
It is told by a Lakota girl who confronts the onslaught of warfare, new technology,
and cultural upheaval in the late nineteenth century. It is dedicated to all the
courageous young women who journeyed to the Carlisle Indian School,
with only a blanket of dreams to shield them in a strange and hostile world.

Published in 1995 by Thomasson-Grant, Inc.
Copyright © 1995
Jewel H. Grutman and Gay Matthaei, authors.
Adam Cvijanovic, artist.
Created in consultation with Arthur Amiotte,
Lakota Studies professor and Oglala Lakota tribal member.
Deborah H. Sussman, editor.
Lisa Lytton-Smith, designer.

Printed in Singapore.

Inquiries should be directed to:
Thomasson-Grant, Inc.
One Morton Drive, Suite 500
Charlottesville, Virginia 22903-6806

00  99  98  97  96  95   5  4  3  2  1

Library of Congress Cataloging-in-Publication Data

Matthaei, Gay.
    The journal of Julia Singing Bear / Gay Matthaei and Jewel Grutman ;
illustrations by Adam Cvijanovic.
        p.  cm.
    A sequel to: The ledgerbook of Thomas Blue Eagle.
    Summary: A Lakota girl of the late nineteenth century tells of her childhood
on the plains and her experiences at the Carlisle School, where she learns the
ways of the white world.
    ISBN 1-56566-095-1
    1. Dakota Indians—Juvenile fiction.  [1. Dakota Indians—Fiction.  2. Indians of
North America—Fiction.  3. United States Indian School (Carlisle, Pa.)—Fiction.]
I. Grutman, Jewel H.  II. Cvijanovic, Adam, 1960-   ill.  III. Title
    PZ7.M43167Jo  1995
    [Fic]—dc20                                                            95-31738
                                                                              CIP
                                                                              AC